MR. HARDING'S
OREGON TRAIL ADVENTURE

The Letters Through Time Series

Ellen Anthony

Published by LN Books Limited
4500 Cannon Avenue #63
Klamath Falls, OR 97603

ISBN-13: 978-1-948168-00-7

FOREWORD

This book is John Harding's account of the same Oregon Trail journey documented by his two children in *Lura's Oregon Trail Adventure* and *Jacob's Oregon Trail Adventure*. Why three books? His ten-year-old daughter and fourteen-year-old son weren't aware of a lot of stuff that concerned the adults and they wrote about what did concern them. John's account has more detail and sheds more light on his children's activities.

IN MEMORIAM

This book is dedicated to my mother, Virginia Anthony, who previewed this manuscript in letter form and saved them all.

Table of Contents

Letter 1

March 1, 1850
Greenfield, Tennessee

Dear Friend:

I am John Andrew Harding. I know you don't know me, but I've been paid a mighty good sum to write to you about the journey my family and I are about to take. We are going to Oregon.

You might ask why. The farm I've owned here in Tennessee is plumb wore out. Three years of bad crops and trying to pay my debts showed me that. You can't keep planting corn and wheat year after year and expect anything to thrive, but they were the only crops that made money enough to satisfy the bank. It's better to just sell up and go where the land is cheap and good.

They say the land in Oregon is the richest there is. I don't believe that but I know it hasn't been touched by the plow and there is good water there. It's a chance to have a bigger and better farm than what I've inherited.

This week I signed the papers and paid my debts. Today Emily and I told the children it's certain and we'll be leaving in a week. That will give us time to pack our farm wagon with our few treasures and time to say goodbye to the friends and family that won't be going.

Thank God Jim has decided to go! My younger brother is a fair shot and a mighty good gunsmith. He sold his land five years ago to our oldest brother, Joshua, and has nothing but his tools to worry about. He's a good farmer too when he sets his mind to it. He plans to buy up some land next to mine in Oregon so we'll have room to expand.

That's important. I only have one son right now but Emily is still young. We plan to have more. Jacob is 14 and has the soul of a farmer. His sisters, Lura and Rachel, are younger. Lura is 10 and Rachel is 6.

I plan to leave Rachel here with her cousins for another year. She's small for a 6-year-old and not as healthy as I'd like. Jim's wife, Elizabeth, will stay too. She's got another baby coming and the trail might be too hard on her. Jim will come back next year and collect them. There's a good chance others from our county will be making the trip them.

Lots of folks are making the journey. Too many are going to California to look for gold, but there's a lot of sensible folk heading for Oregon. Like me they want land and a better future.

Tennessee is just too small to hold us. My family has been here since the 1780s. Back then this was rich land and a man could have as much as he could work and protect. Now the farms are small and wore out and people are moving all the way to Oregon looking for more. That's good because Tennessee is too crowded. Nashville is a city now and folks have been spilling out into the country looking for places to build. Fortunately, Greenfield is too far for most of them.

I worried for a bit that someone would try to plant a town on my hundred acres but it won't happen. Mr. Phillips plans to raise horses here—not good work horses but thoroughbred stock. We talked it over and I expect the land will be better for going to grass. Maybe after a few years of that he'll be able to plant something else.

I know what I did wrong. Planting the same crop year after year isn't good. I actually planted two but I couldn't let fields lie fallow. Not even good cow manure will help after a while. In Oregon I'll be sure to rotate four crops and have some cows on the fallow fields. It's a better way of doing things.

Emily wants to take a few heirlooms with us. Tomorrow we'll be packing the harpsichord into the wagon, then I'll take apart her mother's table and chairs so they'll fit. My plow blade and tools will have to fit too. After that it's just supplies for the trail.

I plan to sell the horses and buy oxen. Horses may be fast but they need too much care and better feed than oxen. Mr. Tillman over in Martin has offered me seven hundred dollars for Banner, my Morgan stud, and another three for my son's mare. The Belgians will fetch good prices too. I'll keep the mules. They'd go for about sixty dollars each and that's not enough.

I'll use the money from the horses to buy supplies. I expect to spend four hundred dollars. I know Emily has some tucked back, but I should have enough without getting into her egg money or the money from the farm.

I'll keep writing to you but this is enough for now. I need to think on what needs to be done.

Sincerely,
John Andrew Harding

Letter 2

March 25, 1850
Independence, Missouri

Dear Friend:

We are in Independence. As I expected it took us three weeks to get here. I didn't push it because there's still ice on the creeks and the roads are muddy. We've had a fair amount of practice getting the wagon unstuck.

One thing we've learned is four oxen per wagon isn't always enough to budge the wheels when they're stuck in gumbo. We're buying extra yokes and the oxen to fill them. It might be better to have eight oxen per wagon anyway. That way we can have four resting and four working most days.

All of us are here. Elizabeth decided to brave the trail with us. Baby or no baby she didn't want to stay behind. We tried to argue her out of it, but Emily said it would make no difference if she stayed or went. If God means this baby to live, it'll happen. If He doesn't, she should be with her family.

That makes sense. Elizabeth has lost four babies in the past six years. The last one looked like it would make it, but was born two months early. This one, if it comes in its proper time, should be born in late September. Hopefully we'll be in Oregon by then.

Rachel is with us too. I couldn't see leaving her behind. She can help her Aunt Bet (that's what the children call Elizabeth) with her chores.

Emily read the last letter before I sent it off and asked me if I was going to say anything about my other daughter. I didn't mean to slight her.

Lura is the clever one. She's just ten, but smart as a whip. She took to reading and writing like she was born to it and I have a hard time staying a step ahead of her. Not that any of my children are slow. Lura just takes a real delight in learning.

I remember when I was that eager. At least I think I do. Emily and I have tried to foster a love of books in our children, but it can be hard. We have very few of our own. The one we read from the most is the Bible. On Sundays it is always the new Testament, but other days I like to read the older stories. We have been reading from Exodus this week because of the journey ahead of us.

I picked up two books in a trade today. We needed blankets and other supplies and we didn't need a second milk cow. Jim's cow is younger and fresher than ours so I traded ours away and picked up two books in the deal. That gives us six.

The shopkeeper claims he's read Ivanhoe and it's good. From what little I read in his store, I'm inclined to agree. The other is one of those plays by William Shakespeare. I've never read a play before, but I've seen bits and pieces of Shakespeare's work. A circus that came through Martin had a couple of actors who did scenes from Hamlet and MacDuff. It was pretty interesting.

Jim did some trading too. He kept most of the guns from his shop until we got here. We figured the prices would be better since most folks preparing for the trail buy goods and guns here. We were right.

After setting up a firing range and showing how accurate his guns were, Jim sold all but three of them. Most of them were old flintlocks he'd added primers to. Some dated back to the War of 1812. A few had rifled barrels. He could have sold more if he'd had pistols or revolvers but what use are those for hunting? Besides the new Colt revolver is what everyone is asking for. I have an Allen pepperbox and my rifle is a Springfield.

Jim didn't sell the Kentucky rifle he'd put back for Jacob. I've paid him for it and my plan was to save it for Jacob's birthday, but I figure he'll need it between. It's a good one with a walnut stock, ramrod and rifled barrel.

We're getting the last of our supplies here. Emily wants to visit the druggist and see what he recommends for the trail. She's worried she won't have something in her medicine chest that she should. I don't think there's anything she can add. Besides dried herbs from her garden, she's got laudanum, Epsom salts, vinegar, baking soda, whiskey, and a bunch of other things. If she could have kept a couple of chickens in there, she'd be happier still.

We left our chickens behind. As much as I like eggs, I can't see chasing those live feather dusters every night. We'll just get a new flock in Oregon.

Shoes. The girls need good shoes. They can't be walking barefoot to Oregon. I need to remind Emily. I just got mine and Jacob's resoled. Maybe Emily needs new ones too. So many things we have to get.

There's an odd herd of people here. Some are farmers but there's a lot more dudes and layabouts. Finding the right train could be an almighty chore. I've been down twice to the courthouse and over to the ferry to see whose putting a train together.

March 27, 1850

I found a notice I like. This one said "Christian families to form a wagon train. No bachelors. Meet this Tuesday, March 27th, at the courthouse meeting room." It was signed by a Mr. Sullivan.

Emily, Jim and I went. There was a crowd there, but a better group than others I'd seen. Mr. Sullivan turned out to be a lawyer. He doesn't want to lead us, but there's a couple of others he thinks might. They've been to Oregon once already.

The crowd was so big they decided on two trains of thirty wagons each. The Sullivan train will leave April 2nd. That's just five days. Those who need a little more time will go with the Brown train. They'll leave on the 5th.

I don't think we'll find a better group. We'll go with the Sullivan train.

March 28, 1850

We met over at the Smith farm today. Mr. Smith has given us room to form our train on his river pasture. It cost us $5 each, but we'll be better organized when we leave. Mr. Tyler arranged that. He's been to Oregon before and came back for his family.

Mr. Sullivan is a fair sort. He's 38, married and has three young boys. Turns out he put up the notice because he couldn't find the kind of company he wanted on a train. It was a good move.

He's bound for Sacramento, California. With all the gold that's been found there, they need lawyers to keep things legal. He sold his practice in Chicago to go west. I'm not sure whether he's a fool for leaving Chicago or brave for wanting to be in California. I think only time will tell. They do need law out there. I'm just not sure California is ready to be a civilized place.

Thirty wagons. Only four bachelors have been let in and they are the brothers and sons of other folk on the train. Then there's a Mrs. O'Leary who has no man, but four daughters and a sister. The sister, Josephine, says she can tend stock and shoot. Jim challenged her and she could.

I'm not so sure they should be making the trip. Without a man they'll be needing help. Those who help might have to neglect their own stock and it just might rile up their wives. Emily would forgive me if I gave them a hand, but I wouldn't do it regular.

Jim brought in a Mr. Watkins and Mr. Thomas to meet me. They are from Kentucky and the closest to being our neighbors. Watkins has a four-year-old girl and a two-year-old boy. Mr. Thomas has six children. They plan to team up like me and Jim. There's also the Parkers and the Courtneys. The Parkers are from Virginia. I haven't caught the names of the rest.

Three days until we leave.

Sincerely,
John Andrew Harding

Letter 3

April 2, 1850
Near New Santa Fe, Missouri

Dear Friend:

On the trail at last! Our first day was uneventful. Of course we've had our little trek from Tennessee to teach us what chores need doing when.

The trickiest thing was the remuda. That's made up of all the spare animals for the entire train. It's pretty big with forty oxen, seven milk cows, four or five mules, and a dozen horses. Handling the animals isn't that hard, but figuring out who should be riding herd caused a few arguments. I finally agreed that someone from one of our wagons will ride after them every day. Between the three of us we can do it and eight of those oxen belong to us. Jim's cow is in with them too.

Mr. Sullivan can't be spared. He's the only man on his wagon. Watkins too. Thomas has a couple of boys who can help, but we need a man riding with them. I'd feel better if there was someone older and wiser riding herd when Jacob does it too. The other wagons will come up with men too.

Rachel is walking barefoot today. Emily said she put her new shoes in the wagon because our youngest nearly left them behind.

April 11, 1850

One of the Courtney boys got shot today. He'll live. His brother got careless while he was cleaning his gun and shot him through the arm. No one in that family knows guns. City folk.

Parker knows one end of a gun from the other. I'll let Jacob ride herd when either Parker or Mr. Thomas are there. One of the Thomas boys joins me when I take my turn and the other teams with Jim. We've got eight men and five boys old enough to ride herd. We could have used a few more bachelors but only if they could ride and shoot. Those on the train can't stick to a horse.

It was made official today that Mr. Tyler would lead us. No one else speaks any Indian and only Jeb Tyler and Bob Hastings have been to Oregon before. Bob gave it over to Jeb Tyler. He knows him and says he's the better man.

Turns out Mr. Tyler went out two years ago as a muleskinner and he's been back and forth on the trail doing that. Now he's bought his land and came back to get his family. Hastings came back with him. He'd hired out to help move a family the year before. This year he's got his mother and kin with him.

If Elizabeth hadn't decided to come this year, I expect Jim would have hired on as a muleskinner or bullwhacker and come back with a freight next spring. Most trains are headed west right now, but I've been told we'll meet freight trains coming the other way. Some of them will sell supplies to those that need them, but not animals. We've been warned about that.

I suppose they are supplying the forts and trading posts on the way. With so many folks headed out to Oregon, they would have to be supplied.

There were four trains preparing to leave Independence on the same day we were. I counted them up and it made 148 wagons. Our train is just 30 of them. If that many leave everyday over the next month, we'll have over 3,000 wagons making the trek. It fair boggles the mind.

I'm glad we left as quick as we did. Good grazing is going to be hard to find for those that follow us. Those that don't leave this month might not find any at all.

Jeb Tyler says we don't need to worry too much about Indians. The route we're taking cuts through a lot of tribal lands, but most of the Indians would rather trade than fight. As long as we keep a strong guard on our stock and stay together, they aren't likely to bother us.

We haven't seen any Indians yet, but we've traveled just about a hundred miles. There's more mud than anything else. Jacob helped Mr. Thomas pull an ox out of a mudhole today. He was a sight to see when he came back. I think he was wearing more mud than the ox.

Al Thomas just grinned and said he let him do the dirty work. That's all right. I'll do the same with one of his boys.

April 12, 1850
 St. Mary's Mission

Rachel, my youngest, has the grippe. So do four others. My girl can't keep her food down so Emily went to the doctor at the mission for advice. He told her bad water probably caused it. No medicine. She's to have tea and dry bread for a day or two. The doctor cost $1.50. We could have saved that.

We're taking a rest day here. With so many people sick, it'll help them. The stock needs the rest anyway.

I've checked out Lura, but she seems all right. She's worried about Rachel, but that's natural. Her eating hasn't slacked off and neither has Jacob's. It's a good thing I shot a deer yesterday so I can feed these two.

I'll send this letter back before we go on.

Sincerely,
John Andrew Harding

Letter 4

Near Scott Spring
April 14, 1850

Dear Friend:

The grippe isn't going to get Rachel. I was plumb worried but caught her in the candy tin tonight. If she can eat candy, she can eat her supper. She needed a paddling but I just asked Elizabeth to take the tin into her wagon. I'm too soft on her, but she's the youngest and so little I can't help it. When she's bigger I'll have to make her behave.

Lura is a lot older and a lot more help. Every morning and night she milks Jim's cow so Elizabeth doesn't have to. She helps set up the bedrolls every night too and washes dishes. I'm not sure what Emily has Rachel doing.

Jacob rides herd and helps with the stock. He's only fourteen, but he knows what he's doing.

April 23, 1850
The Narrows

We started reading *Ivanhoe* today. It's one of those books I got in trade and not a bad one. It's set back when they had those knights in armor. I've heard of them and even saw a suit of armor once at a carnival, but I don't know much about it. The people aren't much different though. There's good people and bad people and people who think they're good because they go to church.

I'm proud to say that my children didn't understand why the other characters were mean to the Jew. They've known Jewish folk like the Bernstein family and didn't think nothing of it. I finally told them that the only true Christian in that book was Ivanhoe. The rest went to church but closed their ears.

We're about a week away from Fort Kearny and I'm concerned about our matches. It's taking more to get a fire going than we thought it would. We need to buy more. We'll be in a sad fix if no one has matches. Jim shares our fire at night and we offer lights to other families that have run out.

Anna Sullivan is one clever cook and she's taught Emily a new way to cook antelope that kills the wild taste and makes it almost good. I gave her a hindquarter of one we shot for payment.

I've made a deal with Frank Sullivan. He was a lawyer back east and doesn't know beans about guns. He can't hunt and I think it would be wrong to teach him. Jim and I will hunt for him and he'll pay us.

April 25, 1850

Rachel has been minding a bit too well and I found out why. We lost a toddler back at the Narrows and it took over an hour to find where she'd wandered off to. Now Betty Downing has to wear a rope when her mom can't watch her.

My smart girl told Rachel she'd be wearing a rope next. I told her she just needed to stay within sight of our wagon and it wouldn't happen. I didn't bother to tell her she's old enough to undo knots.

May 1, 1850
Fort Kearny

I got all the matches I could. Downing wasn't happy because he'd run out completely, but he can light his fire from ours every night. Emily is the best at using matches so she's in charge of the fire now.

Lura got a bucket of milk for milking the cow every morning and night and went off trading. I'm not sure how she did it, but she turned that milk into an apple pie. Emily talked to the soldier's wife she traded with and told me it was a fair deal. The woman just wanted some company for that pie and the milk was just an excuse.

I reckon it's hard for a woman out here. She must be glad to see so many trains going through after a long winter.

There's a mule train getting ready to go east. I'll send our letters off with them.

Sincerely,
John Andrew Harding

Letter 5

May 8, 1850
O'Fallon's Bluffs

Dear Friend:

Now it's colds we're plagued with. Lura and Jim both have them. Emily told me someone would catch cold after we walked in the rain all day. It took three days but she was right. Of course we wouldn't have done it except it looked like the trail would flood.

It looks like it will start raining again. I've got Jacob prodding Jim's oxen and Rachel is staying with her aunt. We've made room for Lura and Jim in our wagon where Emily can keep her eye on them.

I'm thankful not to have that cold. Knowing Emily, she'll be dosing the sick ones with vinegar and following that with chicken soup if she can get a chicken.

I think I'll go looking for the chicken. The Parkers have some and I've seen some over at the Burns' wagon. Maybe I can trade them some meat for one of their birds.

Jim hates vinegar. I could bet a double eagle that he swears up a storm before she gets it down him but Emily will win.

May 10, 1850

We saw some Indians today. Jed said they were Cheyenne. They might not have been looking for trouble, but they didn't act friendly. They were following along just out of gunshot range.

We brought in the herd and tied the loose horses to the wagons. Every man and boy who could handle a rifle had one. The women and children stayed on the wagons.

It was enough. After an hour or so the Indians quit following us. They were looking for easy pickings and we weren't. They were probably looking to steal some horses.

We're mounting a double guard tonight. I've told Jacob to keep it quiet so the girls sleep. He'll take the early watch and I'll take the late one. Jim had better sleep through. His cold is better, but I want him over it. I'll break out the whiskey tonight and give him another dose.

Jacob can pair up with Al Thomas. He's a good man.

May 11, 1850

Jim is back in his own wagon. Three days of chicken soup and vinegar and he swears he's over it. I think he pretty much is. I caught him coughing once out of Emily's sight and it sounded better. Gave him another slug of whiskey to make sure.

Lura's better too. I can't give her whiskey like I'd like. Emily doesn't hold with hard liquor and Lura's too young to keep a secret like that from her ma. Chicken soup and vinegar will have to do the trick for her.

Oh, I got the chicken from the Burns. I owe them an antelope.

May 15, 1850

We lost Anna Sullivan. Her wagon tipped while we were crossing the South Platte and she didn't jump. She got trapped underneath and drowned.

It could have been worse. Jacob got there fast and pulled her youngest boy free. He was on the box with his ma. Carl was scrapped up and scared, but he'll live. Shame about her though. She was a good woman.

Frank is taking it hard. He'll have to get through it.

I went over where the wagon tipped. You see four wagons had already crossed when that wagon went over. It shouldn't have happened. It took a bit but I finally found where the wheel caught. Deep hole. It just swallowed the wheel. We didn't have time to mark it, but I made sure the other wagons in our train avoided it. By the time we were done the Feldman train had come up. They got warned.

May 17, 1850

Today Jim and I decided river crossings are just too risky. We'll take the time to get our women across on the mules before we take the wagons across. Maybe we can get the others to do that.

I got that antelope for the Burns family.
Emily and Elizabeth are helping Frank Sullivan. He's going to need help for a bit.

May 18, 1850

We came across a mule train today headed east. They came out of Fort Laramie. That's the biggest fort on the trail and the best place for us to pick up supplies. I look forward to seeing it.

One of the skinners agreed to post all the letters from our train for a dollar plus the postage. It's a fair price. If you get this one, it's because Jed Dawson lived up to his word.

Sincerely,
John Andrew Harding

Letter 6

May 18, 1850
Ash Hollow

Dear Friend:

Emily has the children writing letters to practice their penmanship. It's good practice and won't do them no harm. Lura takes to it like she does everything, but Jacob is a sight harder to get going. He doesn't mind doing numbers and has a good interest in history, but he doesn't care much for reading and writing.

He'll do all right just so long as he can read and understand what he reads. I've known men who signed bad deals not knowing exactly what they were signing. I don't want that to happen to Jacob.

Not that my son doesn't have a good mind. He's a true farmer and knows about the soil. He just can't sit still for long. Even when we are reading at the nooning, he's got his hands busy with some whittling

Lura is the reader. If I let her have a book all to herself, she'd forget everything till she was done reading. That won't do out here. There's too many things to get done and not that much daylight. Maybe when we get to Oregon, she can lay in bed a day and read, but not now.

I can't recall the last time I had a lie-in. It's just not something you do when you've got work to do and children to raise.

I do remember the last time Emily did it. She had to. Elizabeth had lost another baby and was acting like she was going to die of grief. Emily took to her bed and sent Lura over to proclaim she was dying. I went hunting. I'm not good at lying and Elizabeth would have known Emily was shamming if she'd seen me.

Emily kept Elizabeth and the children busy for two days then Jacob found me and said he knew what was up. It wasn't long after that Elizabeth caught on. She caught Emily with her knitting.

It was a sight to see. I saw Elizabeth storm out of the house then a bit later Emily came across the fields calm as you please looking for me. No sooner had we sat down to supper than Elizabeth came back with Jim. It took a bit to patch things up, but Elizabeth never went back to grieving for that baby.

The nooning is nearly over. The women are finishing up the dishes and we need to yoke the oxen. They are out grazing. Rachel is still napping but she'll wake up in time.

It's three o'clock. We started this one at high noon. Now the chores are done, we've eaten, and the cattle are rested. It's time to move on. The sun sets at half past seven. We'll stop then and set camp while there's still light enough to see. There's only a quarter moon tonight so we'll stay put till near dawn.

The stars are sure beautiful out here on the plains. You can see the Milky Way and the Dipper clear as day. I keep my eye on the North Star. Polaris is what Frank Sullivan calls it. He says all the brightest stars have names, but he has trouble remembering most of them. Figures. I don't think I could remember the fancy names anyway. The North Star works for me.

You can see a lot of stars out here. There's few trees and those we see are always where the water is. This land might be good for grazing cattle someday, but they are going to need a lot more water to grow crops.

Going through this land makes me wonder about Oregon. I've been told it's good farm land, but I need to know about the water. I think I'll go talk to Jeb Tyler tonight. He's been there.

May 20, 1850

Lura's been trading. My smart girl got us some chicken eggs and now there's a cake for supper. I like Emily's cakes. This one is coming out of the dutch oven instead of a proper one, but it'll taste good just the same.

May 22, 1850
Courthouse Rock

We passed Courthouse Rock today. We're making good time. The grass is short though. Either a lot of trains got here first or it hasn't recovered from last year. This area is dry too. I'd hate to see a wildfire sweep through here. There's nothing to stop it.

This could be good farm land if the water holds out. Right now the river is running good, but you can't tell what it's going to be like in July when the runoff is gone.

Patsy lost a shoe today. It's a good thing I packed spares.

May 23, 1850
Near Chimney Rock

The Watkins girl died last night. It may have been cholera. She went to bed a little early and just didn't wake up this morning. We didn't bury her until the nooning because Mrs. Watkins wouldn't let her be.

It's hard to see children go this way. I look at Rachel and think the same thing could happen to her. It's a good thing she's so full of mischief or I might get soft on her.

I have to go hunting yet. Jacob saw some buffalo while he was riding herd. One of those will do us for a while.

May 24, 1850

Got a buffalo yesterday—a nice big bull. There was too much meat for just our wagons so I shared it around. Frank Sullivan helped us butcher and salt it and got a fair share.

I just finished talking to Watkins. He thinks Jacob is trying to steal his dog. I told him that was nonsense, but he went on about it until I offered to buy him.

He shut up. I should take offense but the man just lost his daughter. He's bound to be touchy.

I told Jacob he's not to feed that dog. He swore he hasn't and I believe him.

May 25, 1850
Robidoux Trading Post

We're in the shadow of Scott's Bluff now. We're close to Fort Laramie so I won't bother trading here. There's not much of a choice anyway. We did come across another freight headed east so I'll get this letter posted.

There's good water all along here and plenty of wood for our fires. The grazing is still good too. Some people should settle this land.

Sincerely,
John Andrew Harding

Letter 7

Thunderstorm
May 27, 1850

Dear Friend:

We had a real clapper last night—the biggest, loudest thunderstorm I've ever been in. Circling the wagons and hobbling the horses did no good. The animals stampeded anyway right over the Baker wagon.

We're still putting everything back together. Mr. Downing was killed and has to be buried and one ox had to be butchered (not ours). Several wagons lost their covers and the women and children are looking for them. It took a bit to get the Baker wagon upright again too. Mrs. Baker and her two girls were inside. They weren't hurt much. It's too bad about Downing.

Having those mules was a good thing. Patsy came back on her own. Jacob found the other one pretty quick. Him and that Watkins dog did a fair job of finding our cattle. That milk cow was sure bellering when Lura finally got to milking her.

May 28, 1850
The Laramie River

We sorted out the train today at the Laramie. Some were determined to cross the river, but I'll pay the $1.50 for the ferry. We'll still have to swim the stock across but we won't have to caulk the wagon or worry about accidents.

They need a proper bridge here. There's more than fifty wagons waiting to cross already and another train just arrived. It'll be morning before we get our turn.

I'll while away some time checking the oxen over good and doing some repairs. There's got to be a way to keep the wagon cover from coming loose in a wind.

This valley has good water. It could be good farm land. It's been half cleared already since every wagon that comes through needs firewood and so does the fort. There's not a lot of leavings so I set Jacob to chopping up a good-sized stump.

The fort across the river is plenty big. I can see more than thirty buildings plain as day and there's a tent camp for more soldiers. The trains that have crossed are camping in meadows too.

This is one crowded place. I think we'd better move on tomorrow and get some of these wagons behind us.

Two new wagons want to join us and the O'Leary women are leaving the train. The Carpenters are all right. They wintered here because Mr. Carpenter got work. Now they're ready to move on.

The Foleys are Negro. I've got nothing against that because they are free folk. They come from New York. C. W. said his old train just didn't cotton to them.

I can believe that. Already the Parkers and some others are saying they don't want them.

Foley has offered to be the tail of our train though and that quieted them some.

Jeb Tyler and I went looking for the Foley's old train. Their wagonmaster hemmed and hawed but said Foley was right. Some folks just don't like coloreds. It was nothing he did.

The man should get a chance. I got nothing against free Negroes and neither does Jim. I told Jeb I'd speak for him. There's only him, one son and his wife.

Oh, we also agreed it would be better to move on. There's not enough grazing here. Jeb knows a place just a few miles off the trail that probably hasn't been grazed this year. We'll take a rest day there.

May 29, 1850
Fort Laramie

We swam the stock across this morning then I brought Emily over on one of the mules to get our trading done. By the time our wagon was across we had a keg of pickles, some winter coats and a bit of asparagus. I got enough cash money for my salted meat that it paid for the ferry and the pickles.

Those pickles might taste good. Nothing can beat Emily's home-made ones, but we've run out of those. We'll have to do with store bought until we get to Oregon.

Emily got us some licorice too. That's a treat in these parts. The children fair grinned when she shared it out.

We had the oddest thing happen. Emily asked at the sutler's store for writing paper and there was a parcel there for us. It had the same kind of paper we were given in Tennessee. We had to pay a dollar freight charge but we've got enough writing paper to take us to Oregon now.

Emily says not to fret about it. I think the woman who wanted you to get these letters was a mighty thoughtful person. Thank her for me.

The Foley's wagon was already across. When we moved on they took up the tail. No one said anything today because they didn't want to be there. That wagon gets all the dust and Indians are more likely to pick it off if it lags behind.

That wasn't a fair deal. Sullivan thinks the way I do. He doesn't cotton to being the tail either but he said he'd take his turn if asked.

I'll have to think on it. The man can't shoot.

Sincerely,
John Andrew Harding

Letter 8

May 30, 1850
Register Cliff

Dear Friend:

The late start didn't stop us. We still made the seventeen miles to Register Cliff. This is a real pretty place with good water and better grazing than the fort. There's a big sandstone cliff that overlooks the river and that's what they call the register.

I took the children up there. The cliff is covered with the names of folks that have passed by here. I helped Jacob add ours.

There's one name dated 1822. He must have been a trapper. I can't see someone taking a wagon west that long ago.

The moon is past full but I think it's light enough for a moonlit walk. After the children are to bed, I might persuade Emily to step out with me. She'd like to see this cliff.

June 2, 1850

We are nooning at a place called Washtub Spring. It's a hot spring so the women are all busy doing the laundry and washing the babies.

I took Jacob and Josh Foley hunting. Josh isn't too good with a gun, but he's not green and he's nearly of an age with Jacob. We got some rabbits and roasted them over a fire. With the women doing laundry, we'd better tend to the cooking if we want to eat.

June 3, 1850
Natural Bridge

We found the canyon today. Like Jeb said it hasn't been touched this year. He said he found it when some stock wandered off on his first trip out. It's not easy to see from on top because it's just a big hole in the ground.

We found the draw going down into it and got the wagons down to the water. There's a nice deep creek flowing through the brush and enough grass to keep the animals for several days.

That's not the half of it. This canyon is a pretty sight. It's got bright red walls and, the oddest thing of all, a big stone arch over the water. When we told the children we were staying here for a day, they near shouted with joy. Once their chores were done they went exploring. Jacob took my pepperbox with him and one of the Thomas boys was armed.

This canyon is shaped like a U. We split the train and blocked both ends to keep the stock in.

June 4, 1850

My son is headed for trouble. I saw him up on the bridge last night with that Parker girl. Emily says to leave it alone, but I'm not sure that's wise. Parker is headed for California and that girl is too young to leave him.

No, it won't do. That girl is just thirteen and Jacob is going on fifteen. I'm going to have to keep my son busy I guess.

Frank Sullivan and Amy Downing are courting too. I suspect Emily's been throwing them together but it's not a bad match. She's young and healthy and he needs a mother for his boys. It helps that she can read as good as a school marm. I suspect Frank Sullivan wouldn't look at a woman if she couldn't read to him.

The two of them have been partnering a bit already. He tends her oxen and she's been cooking for both wagons. If it works out, she won't be alone with that little girl of hers.

Jacob and Josh Foley came back with more rabbits. We had a good stew but Emily let them know no more rabbits. If they can't get something bigger, she'll feed us some of that salted meat.

Mary Foley didn't know much about rabbits. It seems she was born in New York City and never had one before. She was a cook in some nice houses and knows fancy dishes, but not rabbit. Emily is teaching her some. She has to know about rabbit fever. That's why we didn't hunt rabbits earlier. They aren't safe in the spring.

I suppose I should say something about darkies and why I don't hold anything against the Foleys. You see a slave ain't the same as a free man. They're lazy. They know they're going to get fed even if they duck work. You have to watch them sharper than a mule to get a fair day's work out of them.

Now a free Negro knows he's got to work as hard as a white man or he doesn't get paid. Not all of them know it, but if they've been free for a few years they've gotten over being lazy.

I've borrowed a slave or two when I was desperate for hands and I've hired free Negroes. I've met many free men who worked as hard as me and a few I've had to run off my place for laying about. I've never met a slave who was worth anything.

Emily feels the same way even though she had a mammy when she was a girl. Her father didn't hold with owning slaves but had no choice when that one came home with his wife. She'd traded her riding horse for the girl who was being whipped something awful. Even after he freed her that black mammy stayed with the family until she died an old woman. I won't say anything against her because she raised my Emily right.

The Foleys deserve a fair chance.

June 6, 1850

We left the canyon today and made our way back to the Platte. The animals are lively and all the better for the rest.

I've got Josh Foley riding herd with Jacob now. He's not a good rider, but he'll keep Jacob from spending too much time with that Parker girl. If I know Parker, he won't let his girl near that colored boy.

Parker is the type who'd own a slave if he could but probably never had the money. I'd feel bad for any slave he did own. I've seen how he treats his stock.

June 7, 1850

We found a ferry run by the Mormons and took it across the Platte. There was a trading post too. We'll mail our letters from there.

This is bear country. I wanted to see what C. W. could do with a gun so we went bear hunting. Bears are tricky to hunt. If you wound one, they're more likely to turn on you than run. You have to be sure of your shot and even then you want someone else standing by with a loaded rifle to help out.

I got lucky and dropped mine. C. W. got off a good first shot, but it didn't kill the bear. Jim was ready to shoot when C. W. let go on his second barrel. It was a decent shot. Foley is steady and a better shot than most city folks.

Frank helped us salt the meat again and I sold him a quarter of my bear for ten dollars. Amy Downing helped.

Time to get this letter to the post.

Sincerely,
John Andrew Harding

Letter 9

Independence Rock
June 10, 1850

Dear Friend:

Have you ever had your boys do a stupid thing? Jacob caught himself a bull snake yesterday. That was all right. I've done that myself and even corked it up in a jar like he did. Letting it loose in the wagon took some doing though. I thought we'd never get his sisters settled down after that snake slithered across their feet.

Rachel woke up three wagons with her screaming and not even Lura would stay in the wagon till that snake was caught. What could I do but tell Jacob to find it even if it took all night? It wasn't easy to sleep with him banging stuff around over our heads and cussing but I managed. I suppose Emily and I could have slept over by Jim's wagon. I didn't think of it last night.

I asked Jacob why he did it this morning and he said Josh was afraid of snakes and he wanted to show him a harmless one. He's not to bring any more back to the wagon.

June 11, 1850

We made Independence Rock today. Jeb Tyler kept warning us we had to be here by the 4th of July if we were going to beat the snows. It looks like we made good time.

The rock isn't anything grand. It's just a huge granite dome. My Lura says it looks like an egg half-buried in the ground. Jacob and Lura climbed it and said there are a couple of trains ahead of us and at least six behind.

We aren't staying long. As soon as the stock are rested, we're pushing on. There's not enough grazing here. There will be less if any of those trains pass us.

June 15, 1850

Jacob is getting good at spotting wild vegetables. Today he came up with asparagus. It was a good-sized patch but old. Asparagus is best before the stems push out from the stalk. Once it branches out and blooms, it takes a lot of boiling and even then it's hard on the jaw. Emily said she'll see what she can do with this batch.

We went hunting too. Jacob brought down a buck deer and showed Josh how to clean it. You can tell he's a city boy. Josh is awfully finicky about blood on his hands.

C. W. has no problem. He said something about slaughtering pigs when he was young then shut up. That makes me wonder. C. W. is a fine-looking Negro, lighter than most, and it's not hard to figure he's got some other blood in him. I don't see it in his son, but it's there in him. He's a mulatto and he's not easy to forget.

Parker seems to know him. Twice he's wanted Jeb to ask for his papers, but that's not something Jeb was inclined to do. I'm not going to do it either. Parker has been hinting that C. W. is from Virginia and a slave. He hasn't come out and said so to his face but just made sly digs. Al Thomas heard the last one and told him to shut his mouth or challenge him.

Parker didn't cotton to dueling with a Negro. He said it wasn't right. I think he just doesn't want to get whipped by a nigger.

Jeb knows what could happen if Parker is right. Bounty hunting. An escaped slave is worth money. If he could drag a slave back to his owner, he might get $500. The problem is he could get a hundred just for bringing back proof that the runaway was dead.

It might not matter to Parker that he'd have to go all the way back to Virginia to get that money, but it matters to me. We aren't turning back and no one on this train is going to do murder for a hundred dollars.

June 16, 1850
Sweetwater River

We're spending the day crossing the Sweetwater. Half a dozen wagons got stuck and we had to work at it. The Foley wagon had to be double-teamed to get it out.

I saw Jacob over at the Parker wagon again. He didn't stay long because he had Josh Foley with him. Good. I wonder what that little girl is telling him about the Foleys.

We have to cross the Sweetwater two more times. We might get the second crossing done today, but the third will have to be tomorrow. There are no bridges or ferries here.

June 17, 1850

Debbie Parker is dead. She got crushed by a wagon wheel. I have to see to Jacob. He's taking it hard.

June 18, 1850

God knows I didn't want that girl dead.

Jacob's in a bad way. I put him to tending Jim's oxen so the girls won't see him. Elizabeth will keep an eye on him while Jim's riding herd.

Jim thinks I should tell him about my first girl. I may have to. The problem is his mother doesn't know about Mattie and I don't feel right telling him before Emily knows.

I might have to come clean to both. Maybe tonight Emily and I can take a walk.

June 19, 1850
Ice Spring Slough

Emily took it better than I thought she would. It's been more than 20 years since I ran away with Mattie Jackson, but you never know how women think about these things.

We were just young-uns. Mattie was a pretty thing and we wanted to marry, but her folks wouldn't let us. When they said they were going to move to Kentucky, we ran away.

We didn't get far before my pa caught up with us. It was just as well. I wouldn't have met Emily if I'd kept Mattie. She's the love of my life.

I'm going to end this for a while and go talk to Jacob. We're camping here tonight because the grazing is good and there's water. I think I'll have time for a long talk.

June 20, 1850

The Parkers are turning back. We tried to talk them out of it, but they have had enough. The Courtneys are going too. So long as they stick to the trail, they'll be all right.

I hope they settle at one of the forts and finish the trip next year. I can understand, though, how they feel. The Parkers have had more than their share of grief.

Courtney has agreed to take our letters back. If you get this one all right, it'll mean they're safe.

Rachel brought me a bucket of dirty white ice last night. It seems she dug it out of the ground. It was nice of her to do it herself. It tasted real good in the coffee.

Sincerely,
John Andrew Harding

Letter 10

The Foleys
June 23, 1850

Dear Friend:

The Foley's wagon tipped again. I think it's the fault of the wagon. They have one of those Conestogas. Of course, it didn't help that they tried to use seven oxen when they pulled it up the ridge. That put the whole thing off balance.

June 25, 1850

We got us a problem. Parker was right. Jacob got the story out of Josh and now we have to do something about it. Jim and I are going to talk to Frank Sullivan. It's better to leave Jeb out of this until we know what we're going to do.

There's nothing we can do tonight. It will have to wait until the nooning tomorrow. It's just bad luck Parker recognized him. He's gone now, but this could come back to us.

June 26, 1850

Josh had the story wrong. That slave Parker talked about escaped in 1840. C. W. produced his manumission papers and his marriage lines to show he'd been free since '35. He said he didn't have a Georgia accent because he didn't live long in Georgia.

I don't know if his story is bunkum or not, but it's not my funeral. Frank looked over his papers and said everything was in order. I told Jacob not to mention it again.

A lot of ruckus over nothing.

June 27, 1850

Lura's got a birthday coming soon. It won't be much of one because we are on the trail, but we've cooked up a surprise for her. I know Jacob is whittling her a doll and Emily is conniving with Elizabeth and Amy Downing.

I've got the hard part. Lura is dropping hints four or five times a day that her birthday is coming and I have to ignore it. It's worse when Rachel starts talking about her last birthday. It was in March and I know we spoiled her. Everyone knew we were going to Oregon so her shindig was big. All our neighbors came and we carried on until folks had to go home for the milking.

The story gets grander every time Rachel tells it and Lura gets teary-eyed. The funny thing is I don't remember half of what she says and I know Emily put her to bed before we broke out the old orchard and the real frolic started.

When she went on about some varmints caterwauling outside her window though, I had to talk to Jim. That I remember. We'd better not get that drunk again.

June 28, 1850
South Pass

Lura is riding on the Sullivan wagon today and taking care of the youngest boy. That keeps her out of the way. Frank can use a hand with that little one anyway. I think the Downing girl is riding with them too. She and little Carl are like twins these days.

Jacob asked me if Lura could ride herd with him as part of her birthday present. I don't see no harm in it. Lura is a fair rider and Al Thomas will be out there too. It'll be nice for Jacob to spend time with his sister. They'd better tend to business though. It won't do to be losing stock while they are carrying on.

June 29, 1850
Pacific Springs

Lura's birthday was today. She looked so miserable I nearly spoiled it but we held out until the nooning. While she was fetching water Emily brought out the cake and presents. Lura's surprise was a sight to see.

We came up with some pretty good gifts. I had a little mirror tucked back into the harpsichord for most of the trip and Emily had ribbons and a bit of candy for our girl. Jacob had that doll he whittled, but Lura liked the idea of riding herd with him even better.

Frank Sullivan surprised me by giving Lura a book. It had belonged to his wife and I suspect he wanted it gone now that he's going to remarry. He couldn't have given Lura a better gift. I suspect she'll be reading it every time she gets a chance.

I'm not sure I want to read this one. It's written by a woman and a young one at that. She was English too. I've looked at a couple of penny-dreadfuls and they are enough to make a man blush. Frank says this one isn't like that, but I may take a look at it. It won't do for Lura to be reading that sort of stuff. She's too young.

Maybe you know this book. Frank says it's a popular one and a lot of people, men too, cotton to it. Have you ever heard of *Frankenstein*?

Sincerely,
John Andrew Harding

Letter 11

Parting of the Ways
June 30, 1850

Dear Friend,

Raspberry cobbler tonight. Jacob and Lura found raspberry bushes and let the train know. I suspect they ate more than they picked because they weren't hungry tonight.

Jacob said they saw a couple of Indians too. They weren't any trouble but he figured they wanted the raspberries so they left a fair share on the bushes. That was good. Those Indians don't own the land, but they have as much a right as we do to what grows on it.

Lura was really tired and happy tonight. She had such a good day that I felt it was time to look at that book of hers. I'll just read a bit after the children go to bed. It won't be long because I don't like wasting lamp oil.

July 1, 1850

This is where our train splits. Ten wagons are going to California and the rest of us, nineteen wagons, are going to Oregon. It'll take a bit to sort everything out and say our goodbyes. We've got a wedding to do too. Frank Sullivan and Amy Downing are making a match.

There's no parson on our train. I've been speaking at funerals, but this is different. The

Sullivans need a better send off than I can give them. There's another train behind us and I've a mind to see if they have a parson.

I worry that some folks going to California will catch that gold fever. I've heard of men ruined by that dust and I hate to think certain folks might do the same. Not Frank Sullivan, but others.

Land is worth more than a bit of gold. Good farm land will feed families, clothe them, and give them a comfortable living. Gold is no good to eat and it spends too easily. Those that chase it are likely to starve when the snow hits.

It won't do no good to warn them and it ain't my funeral. I'd better tend to my own business and let our friends alone.

We need to finish Ivanhoe today. We've been reading it for weeks, but we're so close to the end now it would be a shame to leave off now. The Sullivans and the Foleys have been joining us although the Foleys don't read.

Better see if I can find that parson first. It's already been decided that we'll take a rest day here while the train is being sorted out.

July 2, 1850

I couldn't find a parson so the Sullivans married country style. I said a few words and so did Al Thomas before Frank and Amy jumped the broom. Frank said that would do until they got settled in California and could find a preacher.

They've got more than fifty witnesses so it's nice and legal. It's not as good as a church wedding, but folks can't always do that. I'm sure God understands.

Last night got a bit rowdy but today we are back to business. The trains are sorted out and I've finished with Ivanhoe.

I had to thank Frank Sullivan for that book. I've only read the first four chapters but it's uncommonly good. I'm not sure Lura will like it, but I'm not ashamed to admit I'm going to read the whole thing. It sure is different. It's hard to believe that a woman wrote it.

Ivanhoe was different too. It got us thinking how lucky we are to live in a democracy. The story came out all right, but Frank and Elizabeth both said that good King Richard died after it and the English had to crown that Prince John.

Not good. I'm glad it can't happen here. We've had a president die in office but our founding fathers planned for that. By the time we'd heard that President Harrison had died John Tyler was sworn in. Even though it had never happened before, it didn't seem that there was much confusion.

I voted for Harrison and didn't like Tyler much at the time. He turned out to be a good president, but you never know. I did learn to pay attention to who might be vice president. Our current president, Zachary Taylor, is good but I don't care for his vice president. Fillmore is a politician through and through. I prefer military men. They know the cost of war.

If I had my way, I'd want every president to be a military man. War is a serious thing and until a man has had to face it himself, he doesn't know how serious it is. I know we will have to fight wars to keep our country free, but the man at the top should know who is doing the fighting and what it's like.

Frank doesn't agree with me. He thinks a good knowledge of the Constitution and the law are more important. It's not surprising for a lawyer to say that. He can have his views. It makes for a lively discussion.

I'm going to read more of Lura's book later. I wish there was a full moon, but it's past. I'll just have to stop when it gets dark.

July 3, 1850

We left the Parting of the Ways today. The California train left before we did. They'll join up with a larger train when they get a chance.

The Sullivans will be settling in Sacramento. Once we're settled, I'll send a letter off to them. I'd like to stay in touch.

Sincerely,
John Andrew Harding

Letter 12

July 4, 1850
Green River

Dear Friend:

Today was Independence Day. We didn't have gunpowder to spare and no crackers, but we celebrated just the same. All day long you could hear folks singing Yankee Doodle.

We had a church service at the nooning to thank God for this great country. Of course, he had a lot of help from some mighty good men.

We reached the Green River before nightfall and there was some good grazing left. Folks on the Feldman train got there first and tried to keep our stock off it, but we patched it up. Jeb and their captain dickered a bit.

The Feldman train has been ahead of us since Natural Bridge. It's pretty small now because most of their wagons went to California. Jeb asked if they wanted to join their six wagons with us, but they voted it down.

There's safety in numbers. We haven't had any problems with Indians yet, but it could happen. Jeb tells me we are entering Shoshone lands now. Like the Cheyenne, they mostly let settlers cross their lands so long as no one tries to stay here. That doesn't mean they won't steal from us though. We have to keep a sharp eye on the stock.

Lura found us a bag of cornmeal. She traded a bucket of milk for it. We get plenty of milk and butter from Jim's cow, but other things are coming up short. Emily keeps telling me she needs eggs, but we can't help it now.

The Burns wagon had chickens but the last one died over a week ago. No one else had more than four and they're all gone now. Until we get to a fort no eggs and no chickens.

I'd like a good plate of flapjacks with real maple syrup or even molasses on them. Of course, it wouldn't be right without a fried egg and bacon to finish with. It does no good to dream about it. Emily will make up some corn meal mush tonight and we'll have it fried tomorrow. It's not quite the same as we had at home, but Emily makes it tasty.

The women folk have their chores all figured out. In the morning Emily lights the fire and cooks breakfast while Elizabeth gets things together for the noon meal, puts stuff away, and makes sure nothing is forgot.

At the nooning Elizabeth does the cooking. If we have water handy, Emily does laundry and dishes from breakfast and gets a few things together for the evening meal. In the evening they work together. Sometimes I keep Emily company during the dishes. Other times Jim helps his wife.

I know most families would make the children do the dishes all the time, but that ain't sporting. Besides any time we let them off, they are quick to disappear and we can have a bit without them underfoot.

Getting time alone with my wife is an almighty trial. Last time we managed it was back at Natural Bridge. Even then we had to be quiet about it.

When we reach Oregon I'm going to find us a hotel room and leave the children with Jim. It'll just be one night, but it's going to be a night to remember!

July 5, 1850

I tipped the wagon today and now we're short of gunpowder. One of the kegs broke open and I couldn't save much. Emily found out at the nooning we lost most of the bacon too. That's made her mad. Most of the wild meat we get tastes better with bacon cooked on the top. There's just not enough fat without the bacon.

July 6, 1850

Jeb says we've traveled a thousand miles now and we're more than halfway to Oregon. We should be at Emigrant Springs tomorrow.

Both girls are sleeping in the wagon now. We've used enough supplies that they can make decent beds. I set Jacob to guard duty in the early part of the night, but it didn't do no good. Rachel was up and down and Emily got skittish.

July 9, 1850

Got a king elk today with the biggest set of antlers I've ever seen. I don't usually keep racks, but these will make a mighty fine gun rack. They went into the wagon.

We're going to have to build a lot of furniture or trade for it in Oregon. Beds are no problem so long as we can rope them. If the ropes are tight and there are plenty of them, they'll be comfortable. All you need is a good number of quilts and feather beds to make them good. Of course, we've been sleeping on hard ground for months. Any padding will be welcome.

July 10, 1850

Jeb lost a horse today. He had three when we started, but now there's just two. It was a pretty good mare, nearly the best on the train, and I can see why some young buck took a fancy to it.

He was clever and snatched that mare nearly out from under Jacob's nose. I'm glad Al Thomas was there to keep my son from chasing that Indian down. I've heard those Indians aren't alone. Sometimes they've got friends ready to steal the horse of anyone following the first. Jacob was riding our mule, but Patsy can run. If he'd caught up with that gray mare, I'm sure some buck would forget she was a mule.

Jeb told Jacob to forget it. He'd brought that mare along because she looked good and he figured someone would take her. He told me later that he'd won her in a poker game. Until his first horse broke his leg, he hadn't even ridden her much. She had some bad habits and he hadn't had time to break her of them.

July 11, 1850
Smith Trading Post

We floated the wagon across Thomas Fork yesterday then came here in time for the nooning. Fifteen dollars for a keg of gunpowder! That's robbery, but there's nothing I can do about it. The bacon cost us two dollars. Emily was ready to do without when she saw that price. It's not likely to cost us less at Fort Hall. That's our next big stop. I told her we'd better get it now because the prices are getting higher the further we go. Back in Tennessee the bacon would have been thirty-five cents for a five pound slab. The gunpowder was six dollars a keg.

Sincerely,
John Andrew Harding

Letter 13

Near Soda Springs
July 12, 1850

Dear Friend,

We went hunting yesterday and got a wild goat. It was a good shot, but that son still managed to jump a ravine before it died. I was sorely tempted to leave it. Jacob was with me though so we climbed down the ravine and up the other side to get it. Emily was fit to be tied when we came back so long after dark.

I kept wishing for a good moon, but it's just a little sickle moon right now. It was hard to see those rocks in the dark. We didn't have a lantern with us so we had to make do with a pine torch.

We cleaned and skinned the goat last night and cut it up today during the nooning. Salted some of it, cooked some, and traded some. The Watkins were low on meat and they have to feed that dog of theirs.

July 14, 1850

Dust storm today. It died down after we reached this place. There's good water of which I'm glad. It took nearly a bucketful to get the grit out of my mouth and I know the oxen are feeling it worse. One of them, the spotted one I bought back in Independence, has been losing weight faster than the others. I told Jacob to keep him with the loose animals for the next three days. I'm hoping the rest will do him good.

I don't name oxen. They aren't as smart as horses and a name would just confuse them. If they remember the commands, it's as much as can be hoped for. They are strong though. We had the O'Learys drop from the train back at Fort Laramie because they had horses, not oxen. They didn't get far at all. We've got another wagon, the Baker one, that has mules. They've lost three so far and I think a fourth is suffering. They should trade them off and get oxen before we make the climb into the mountains.

Jacob and the girls brought in some fresh trout for dinner. The fishing is pretty good here, but the land has been over grazed. We'll move on in the morning.

July 16, 1850

Rachel is sick again. Emily thinks it was the water. Maybe so.

I finished Frankenstein and let Lura know I approved it. We started reading Romeo & Juliet with the others today.

July 17, 1850

Rachel is better. I had to put down that spotted ox. We debated whether to take the meat, but it's probably safe. We'll cook it good just in case. I think it was just wore out.

We had to burn one of Emily's chairs tonight. There was no firewood left with so many trains going through here each year. Watkins and Thomas dug out some wood too. Between the three of us we got a fire that lasted long enough to cook dinner.

Early night tonight for the women and children. Jacob is taking the early watch and I'll relieve him before midnight. Thomas shares his watch and one of his sons will join me.

July 18, 1850

Sometimes you shouldn't help. The Watkins wagon needed a new axle and I had a couple of spares. I didn't know when I offered one that Nathan would insist on trading that dog of his for it.

Don't get me wrong. That Shiner is a good cattle dog and he works well with Jacob, but he doesn't belong to us. Still I couldn't refuse the dog. They needed the axle. We couldn't leave them out here.

Jacob was ready to give the dog back then and there, but that wouldn't do. Until we get some place where the Watkins can trade something, we'll have to let it be. The deal is done.

July 19, 1850

Rachel is back to herself. She's been playing with that dog and even tried to get him up on the wagon. He had more sense than to go.

Lura is up to something. I thought she was reading that book of hers, but Elizabeth tells me she's sewing. That's got me worried. Lura doesn't like to sew even though Emily made sure she knows how.

July 20, 1850

My smart girl has a trade in mind. I got it out of her today while we were walking. It may not work and I made her promise to take Jim or me with her when she tries it. She's working on a rag doll.

Romeo & Juliet is sure different. The language is hard to read, but the story is pretty clear—two families feuding and no one remembers why. That sounds like a feud I heard about in eastern Tennessee. No one knows why the McCoys hate the Hatfields, but it sounds the same as this one. It's not a good thing to hold a grudge like that. The poison spreads faster than a snakebite.

July 21, 1850
Fort Hall

It worked. I figured there would be an Indian village at Fort Hall, but I didn't think Lura would actually manage to trade a little rag doll for a half-grown dog.

Jim said he just tagged along to make sure Lura was safe. My girl walked around the village until she saw a dog she liked and a little girl with her papa and started dickering.

The Indian was so surprised to be dealing with a girl he listened to her. Jim said he didn't speak much English, but he understood Lura wanted the pup and was offering the rag doll in trade. Before they got done there was a whole mess of Indians there watching Lura make this trade.

My girl is fearless. If they'd been in a fighting mood, Jim couldn't have done a thing but she just kept on talking and motioning from the doll to the Indian girl to the pup. She got it done.

Jim thinks they enjoyed the show. He figures it was the first time a little white girl had ever settled their hash. She didn't speak any Indian and couldn't pronounce the name of the pup they gave her. Jim can, but he had to repeat it several times.

Now she's traded the pup to Jacob for the Watkins' dog.

She wants to get Shiner back to the Watkins, but it may take a while. I told her it's got to be a fair trade or they won't go for it. Nathan Watkins has pride.

Sincerely,
John Andrew Harding

Letter 14

July 23, 1850
American Falls

Dear Friend,

We left Fort Hall a couple of days ago. There wasn't enough grazing there and too many trains coming in. This place has enough grazing and we're letting the animals eat and rest up for a day. The children have been fishing again and I'm fixing a few things.

The moon is close to full. When we move on we won't have to wait for daylight.

Jacob is using Shiner to train that pup. He's a scrawny dog. Like most Indian dogs he's probably had to steal what he could from the scraps his owners leave. Getting rewarded with bits of meat for doing things is new to him. He's catching on fast though.

July 25, 1850

We left the falls close to dawn this morning then stopped for a long nooning. Al Thomas spotted a clump of raspberry bushes. These are even better than the last ones. Jacob said the berries were so ripe they just slid into his hands.

July 26, 1850
Raft River

This is Jacob. Pa's been bit by a rattlesnake. He'll live, but Ma says he can't write for a few days and I should do it for him.

The rattlesnake got his hand. Uncle Jim was there and sucked out the poison, but it's still swollen up three times its size. Pa has it soaking in Epsom salts.

He'll be all right.

July 27, 1850

Pa is fevered today. His hand is smaller, but he's out of his head right now. Ma doesn't think jolting him around in a wagon will help.

Uncle Jim says we are going to stay here at Raft River. He gave me Pa's pepperbox to carry because the train is moving on. The Bakers, Mr. Thomas, and Mr. Watkins are staying with us. We won't be alone.

July 28, 1850

Pa is better. He's not raving any more. We had to move on. Lura rode in the wagon with Pa. He'll be all right. He just needs time to get over this.

July 29, 1850

Now it's mosquitos! Those gallnippers fair drove me crazy today. Ma told Pa to stay in the wagon or she'd dose him with laudanum. He wanted to ride one of the mules.

Pa will be all right.

July 30, 1850
Caldron Linn

This is John. My hand's still mighty sore. I've asked Emily to write this for me.

We met up with the rest of the wagon train here at Caldron Linn. They waited for us. We'll go on together.

About that rattlesnake. I was lucky it just caught my hand. I didn't see it and it didn't rattle till after it struck. It happens that way sometimes. Anyway, it didn't kill me. My hand still has some swelling, but I can move my fingers.

I see Jacob did a fair job of keeping up the letters.

Your next letter will be longer. I just can't think that well right now.

Sincerely,
John Andrew Harding

Letter 15

Near Three Islands
August 1, 1850

Dear Friend,

I think I'll live. Today was the first day it didn't hurt to move my fingers. Emily is still insisting I ride the wagon or one of the mules, but I took over some of my chores today. I had to. The girls have been looking scared ever since that snake bit me. They've seen too many others die.

I thought I was going to. I'm still a bit peaked, but a lot better than I was. I had time enough to reflect on my sins, though, while I was waiting. There's a few things I need to set straight and a few fences I need to mend. I'm thankful the Lord has given me time to do it.

My older brother, Joshua, was almighty angry when I sold the farm and it wasn't to him. I tried to tell him the soil was wore out and he didn't want it, but I think I'd better write him a letter and tell him again. Maybe in a year or two he'll sell up and come out to Oregon. I don't want him thinking I sold that land to the highest bidder.

Then there's you. I lied to you and I did my son an injustice. He was right about C. W. and I lied about it. I guess I was just trying to protect the man.

It doesn't matter now. C. W. had papers but they weren't good enough. Frank Sullivan drew up new papers. Now C. W. is from Tennessee instead of Georgia and the difference between a Virginia and a Tennessee accent ain't that much. Unless someone hauls him in front of a certain judge in a certain city, they won't be able to tell his papers aren't real. I know the judge and he's not likely to deny signing the papers once he knows a man's life is on the line.

C. W. told me he married Josh's mother when the boy was two. He said he couldn't have children of his own and the boy needed a father. The real C. W. was a friend of his and wouldn't mind that he'd taken on his name. He died on the docks.

I knew C. W. was a dock worker. It's not surprising he gave that up. If there's a more dangerous way to make a living, I don't know about it. Well, coal mining maybe.

I just wanted to set that straight. Emily is glaring at me so I think I'll stop now.

August 2, 1850

Elizabeth just had her baby. It's a boy.

She picked a pretty place to have him. We're on the Snake River at a place called the Upper Salmon Falls. This whole canyon is full of waterfalls.

They named the boy Adam Joshua Harding.

August 3, 1850
Three Islands

I tended the oxen today.

Adam's a bit small. I'd wager he's less than five pounds. Rachel was about the same size when she came, but she didn't waste breath crying like this one does. She hollered when she was born, of course, but this one tries to cry when he's got no breath left. That's not a good sign.

The women folk came over to see him at the nooning. I could just hear them clucking over this and that. I kept busy caulking the wagon with Jacob. We have to ford the Snake River here.

Emily told me she's going to sleep with Elizabeth tonight. She needs help with the baby.

August 4, 1850

We found a hot springs today. The women called a halt so they could do laundry. Jacob's gone off with some other boys to swim. I expect I'll follow him soon.

The baby made it through the night. Jim knows he's hurting. Something is wrong with him, but I'll be dashed if I know what it is. His limbs are straight.

August 5, 1850

I'm real proud of my Lura. She traded Shiner back to Mrs. Watkins today. She's a clever one, my Lura. I just wish she hadn't traded for an Indian cradle board.

Elizabeth put a brave face on it, but she knows this baby isn't going to need it.

I wonder where the Watkins got that board? It's a pretty thing made of soft buckskin leather and beaded down the center and on the edges. Really fine work.

Jim is hoping there's a doctor at Fort Boise. The baby is three days old now. If he can hold on another two or three days, there might be a chance.

August 6, 1850

Mountain lion. Jim saw some tracks while he was hunting with Jacob and Nathan Watkins. Jeb came back from his hunt and said he saw sign too.

I didn't go. It took a bit of convincing to get Jim to go but we needed the meat. It didn't do any good. They didn't see anything bigger than a rabbit. This whole area might be over hunted between the mountain lions and the people passing through. The grazing is good and that tells me the animals that should be here have moved out and the people passing through haven't lingered. I know we'll move on as soon as it's light.

I started reading again tonight. We had to build up a fire to keep the mountain lions away so it would have been a shame to waste it.

Lura did a fair part of the reading. She likes Juliet's nurse and some roughs were teasing her. Jacob and Jim read their parts.

I'd never read a stage play before. It's easier than a book to pass around and share with others. I can see why people enjoy them.

I can't say I like where this play is going though. This Romeo is just as stupid as I was when I was a boy. He ran off with Juliet and got married. It's too bad no one stopped him like my pa stopped me.

Elizabeth went to bed early. Emily is taking care of the baby so she can rest.

August 7, 1850
Fort Boise

Our nooning was short today. Everyone knew how close we were to the fort and we pressed on quick as we could. Just as soon as we got in sight, Jim and Elizabeth took the mules and went looking for a doctor.

Jacob and I took care of the oxen. There's not a lot of grazing here, but I bought hay to hold them.

This is a pretty good sized fort and there's a town growing up here too. I'm sure Jim will find a doctor. I'd like to find a farrier. Two of our oxen need new shoes and I've run out of spares. If I can I'll trade off the roan ox—the one with the blaze. He's the weakest of the lot.

Jeb took a vote tonight. We'll stay a day here so the animals can be rested and re-shod. We've got some mountains just ahead of us and they need the rest.

Sincerely,
John Andrew Harding

Letter 16

August 8, 1850
Fort Boise

Dear Friend,

Jim decided last night. This morning I had to tell the children that Jim and Elizabeth were going to stay here at Boise. It's the only chance that baby's got to live.

I can't blame them. They've tried for years to get a child and this one has lived the longest. Maybe the doctor is right and he'll come around with lots of rest and a bit of laudanum to ease the pain.

The girls are taking it hard. Jacob is a lot quieter, but I know he's going to miss Jim.

We could stay here till next spring, but I reckon it would be a waste of time for me to stay. I'm a farmer and there's not much else I can hire out to be. Jim is a gunsmith and he's already found work.

No, it would be better if I went on and bought our land. We can start clearing and plowing before Jim gets there. Jim agreed. We're sorting out the oxen so I've got the strongest animals and Jim is going to give me his stake money. I'll put it away in a safe place.

August 9, 1850

Time to leave. Jim saw us off. He said Elizabeth couldn't take saying goodbye to the girls. I don't blame her. Rachel wailed until I told her I'd give her something to cry about. Lura looked like she wanted to. Jacob was glum all day.

We crossed the Blue River today. I'll be teaming with Watkins and Thomas till we reach Oregon. We're less than twenty wagons now, but we've only had four quit along the way and Jim will be coming on next year. I don't know how other trains have done, but I think we've done a fair job of it.

August 10, 1850

The children are still sulking, but they'll get over it. Come spring we'll have Jim and Elizabeth back again.

Don't get me wrong. I miss my brother and would grieve if anything happened to him, but this ain't the same. We're just parted for a while. When the snow melts next year and I start needing help with the planting, he'll be there.

We forded the Malheur River today. I saw more lion tracks. I've told Jacob to keep his rifle loaded and ready. This is pretty country, but it's not where we want to be. We also got warned about the Cayuse Indians. They've burned out people who settled here.

August 11, 1850
Farewell Bend

Bless Sara Watkins! She hired the girls to keep an eye on her toddler. They have to watch Billy Thomas too since both boys play together.

August 12, 1850

Lura saw some fall leaves today. She made me homesick for Tennessee talking about how pretty the trees would be. Jacob told her to shut up.

I don't cotton to him yelling at his sister, but he's right. We need to think about what's before us and not what's behind.

August 13, 1850

Some Cayuse Indians came into camp today to trade. After some thought I traded one of our extra coats for a good supply of fruit. We need that more and I didn't want them to go empty-handed after hearing about them. They minded their manners though.

They told us mountain lions are kind of thick through here. They like cattle.

I can believe that. I went hunting with Jacob and it took us a while to find something worth wasting the powder on. We brought back a small buck deer. Jacob shot it.

August 14, 1850

We broke the wagon tongue today and had to replace it with our spare. It happened at a bad time. Half the train was ahead of us and half behind and nowhere room enough for us to let them through.

August 15, 1850

The gall darnedest thing happened. A mountain lion dashed into camp and made off with Billy Thomas. She took off with him so fast no one could fire a shot.

One moment the boy was playing on a quilt and then that cat had him. She led us on a chase.

That Watkins dog caught her first and latched on to her tail. When she turned to fight we could shoot without hitting the boy, but we nearly got Jacob's pup.

The cat didn't have a chance.

Al grabbed his son and stripped him to see if he was hurt. Nope. He had a few tooth marks, but that cat didn't even break his skin. The boy was stunned, but got over that quick enough when he saw his pa.

That cat was ten foot long from nose to tail. She was nursing too so we found her den and killed her cubs.

When we got back to camp Sara was making a real fuss over Rachel. It seems she threw herself over the Watkins boy when that cat showed up. That was quick thinking. She couldn't save both of them, but she did protect the one.

It's a good thing Billy didn't take any lasting harm. He was back to playing with the Watkins boy before we broke camp.

Sincerely,
John Andrew Harding

Letter 17

August 21, 1850
Umatilla River

Dear Friend,

We didn't do much climbing today and it went quicker, but we'll be climbing again soon enough. We had a long nooning and Jacob helped me with repairs. One of our ropes broke when we were going downhill. The wagon had a drag on it, but losing that rope sure gave us a fright. I have it mended now and it won't break where it broke before. We went over the rope looking for other weak spots. There were a couple we had to fix.

August 22, 1850

Thick fog today. We had to wait for it to burn off so I got Lura talking about Romeo & Juliet. She's been moping about it. My daughter said Juliet should never have met Romeo on the sly when she knew her parents wouldn't approve. I'm glad she thinks that way.

I was curious what Jacob thought since he knows about Mattie. He got all serious and said Romeo was wrong. He was too young, had no property of his own, and couldn't hold on to his temper. When things went wrong, he didn't even go to his folks and tell them about the marriage.

I admit I can see a lot of myself in that young fool. The only thing he did right was not taking Juliet with him when the prince banished him. On the other hand, it might have ended differently if he had.

Emily had her say too. She thought more of the blame should have been had by the nurse and the priest. If they hadn't helped the couple, the marriage wouldn't have happened. When it went wrong they could have stopped it if they'd gone to the prince or owned up to it with the parents.

Lura said something about the prince making sure they stayed married. I didn't cotton to that. I wouldn't want the law telling me my girl had to stay married to a no-account varmint when I'd like to settle his hash.

Lura said she'd only look at guys who have money or land. She was all-fired serious so I couldn't laugh. I wanted to. I'm glad she's only eleven and Rachel's six. I'm not ready for my girls to grow up.

August 23, 1850
Echo Meadows

Nice place. The leaves are really starting to turn. Rachel near drove us crazy yelling so she could hear her echo.

Jacob will be fifteen in a few days. He knows that Kentucky rifle was his birthday present. I wish I had something more, but it will have to wait till we reach Oregon.

Jacob has outgrown his shoes and his feet are bigger than mine now. He still has to wear those shoes, but I'll get him some new ones when I get a chance. It's not healthy to have toes scrunched up.

His pants are mighty short too. Emily noticed. Lura's blue calico dress is pretty worn too. Emily told her not to wear it again till last.

When we get to Oregon, some shopping will have to be done. I hope the prices are better than I think they'll be.

August 26, 1850
McDonald Ford

Jacob got a bear today. One shot. It was a very lucky shot, but a clean one smack dab in the side of the head. It was after an ox. The bear was a big one with over two hundred pounds of meat. We shared the meat around the train since we're getting low on salt. I would have liked to keep the hide, but it would have been more trouble than it's worth right now. We've still got those antlers and I've heard enough complaints about them.

Sara Watkins did some sorting and trading today. Their wagon was so heavy it got stuck in the mud and we had to unpack some to get it out. One trunk came across the river behind Patsy. It was a good water-tight trunk, but heavy. She lightened it up before it went back in the wagon.

August 27, 1850
Biggs Junction

Jacob turned fifteen today. Emily had a pie for him and Lura gave him a collar for the pup. Rachel came up with a shaving mug of all things.

Nathan Watkins said the shaving mug was an extra that Sara threw away back at the ford. I figure Rachel poked through the stuff they tossed.

August 28, 1850
Deschutes River

We passed a group of graves today. We're always passing graves, but these three had the same last name. A family. You have to wonder how it happened. Disease ain't likely—not with adults and children in the same day. We haven't seen a busted up wagon either.

Lura is getting good with the mules. She got Patsy across the river smooth as ice. Emily and Rachel had the other mule. Jacob and I floated the wagon across.

August 29, 1850
Camp Drum

We've reached the Dalles. I had to make a choice today whether to raft the river or take the Barlow Toll Road. Jeb Tyler says rafting will get us there sooner, but I hate paying out $80.00 to save a few days. I thought about building a raft of my own, but that wouldn't save any time and I don't like the looks of that river.

Al Thomas feels the way I do. So does Nathan, but his wife would like him to raft it. There may be enough who want the toll road to make a train. If not, I'll see if anyone is waiting for company. We need at least six wagons.

Sincerely,
John Andrew Harding

Letter 18

August 30, 1850
The Barlow Toll Road

Dear Friend,

We are on our way. A week should see us in Oregon City.

We've got eight wagons. Six are from our old train and we allowed two others to join—the Andersons and the Drakes.

With Jeb gone rafting down the river we needed a new leader. Somehow I got elected.

I'll do my best.

August 31, 1850
Tygh Valley

Jacob complained about Tom Drake today. He's seventeen and looked a fair rider, but Jacob says he was off riding and not minding the herd like he should.

I told him to give him some time. Tom is new to our train.

We don't have much of a herd any more. There are six oxen, no mules besides ours and no spare horses. The oxen are worn down enough that they don't get notions.

Emily traded one of her quilts for a sack of flour. I hated to see her do it, but it wasn't one of her best quilts.

September 1, 1850
Barlow Pass

Just when you think nothing more can happen, it does. I broke my rifle. The wagon tipped and I'd stupidly left the rifle on the box. Now it's in pieces. I doubt even Jim can fix it.

We lost supplies too. A bag of flour tore open and we lost a lot of that.

Jacob offered me his rifle, but that won't do. He's riding herd. I told him I had my pepperbox. It's no good for long shots, but others are armed.

September 3, 1850

The Andersons are gone. I should have noticed sooner. I'm sure Indians didn't get them, but it bothers me that I didn't find out until we made camp. Maybe they had trouble.

The Drakes were surprised too. I didn't find out until today that they only met the Andersons at Camp Drum. I thought they'd come from the same train.

Al suggested they might have seen some likely land. There was some he'd like to check out. Since they didn't have a horse, they might have gone off to check it now. If so, I wish they'd said something first.

Maybe they'll come into camp tonight. There's just a little sliver of a moon but the stars are real bright.

Drake broke out his fiddle and got the young-uns dancing. Jacob paid a little attention to Becky Thomas and the girl was fair beside herself. She's not as pretty as that other girl but I like her family a fair sight better.

The Burns wagon is still with us. They've had their losses, but it ain't over yet. It looks like one of their oxen will die before morning. I traded them one of my spares so they won't lag behind. I got $40 and a sack of flour to replace the one we lost.

September 5, 1850

There's a thief on the train. He didn't get our money but three others—the Drakes, the Watkins, and the Thomas family—were robbed.

We had to unpack the wagons to see what all was missing. Our land money was still tucked into the harpsichord. It's not easy to reach and I think that helped. Emily said her spending money is still safe. I didn't ask where. The money I use for supplies is here too. I checked it when I sold that ox.

I found the pieces of my rifle in the harpsichord. I almost threw them away, but maybe Jim can fix it.

September 6, 1850

It's not on the train. There's over four thousand dollars missing and two rifles. One of those belonged to Al Thomas and the other was Drake's. This is right odd. I've traveled with everyone except the Drakes and I'd say they were guilty if they hadn't lost so much. On the other hand I didn't know Nathan Watkins had more than a thousand dollars tucked away. He's been so tight with his money I didn't think he had any.

I trust Al Thomas and I don't doubt he had the kind of money he says. I have more than two thousand myself and a thousand of Jim's. I'm careful not to ask Emily what she's got. I know it's more than just egg money. Her parents were right generous when she married me and left her some when they died too. We've agreed she should keep it back for the girls when they marry.

We don't know how long the money's been gone. It could be the Andersons took it. They still haven't caught up with us. Drake, Thomas and I are riding back to find them. Watkins will stay here.

September 7, 1850

We found the Andersons. They had a broken axle. Anderson said he walked back to that broken wagon and took one off it.

There's some that wouldn't believe that, but I crept under the wagon and the grease is fresh. The axle is old, but you can still see the fresh scarring made by the tools. He wasn't that good at it.

The problem is I found a rifle tucked up under the box while I was down there. It's an odd place to keep a rifle so I fetched it out. Anderson said he saw it when he changed the axle, but didn't know who put it there or when. He hadn't been under his wagon in weeks.

It was Drake's rifle. As soon as he saw it, he wanted to lynch Anderson but we needed the money back. We only found seventy-five dollars and I have no doubt that belongs to Anderson. He got pretty hot when Drake called him a thief and it got worse when Drake suggested he hid the money back in that broken down wagon.

This isn't good. Anderson strikes me as honest and this whole ruckus smells of skunk. What's worse is two families—the Burns and the Millers—left camp while we were gone. They hadn't lost anything so they went on.

We're going to have to take apart the Anderson wagon and check everything. It will take some time.

We have him. It wasn't Anderson at all, but Tom Drake. Once Al and Nathan told us where they kept their money—under the wagon seat for both—and Drake said he kept his in the same place, it started coming together.

Lura was the key. My smart girl had seen Tom Drake inside the Watkins' wagon. As soon as she said it Tom started to run. One of the Thomas boys tripped him up and Jacob was on him before he got back to his feet.

It took a while, but Tom finally saw it was no use and told his pa where he hid the money. It was back in Tygh Valley. Jacob thought he knew the spot so I sent him off with Al Thomas. I'd better stay here to keep people from lynching Tom. He'll have to stand trial.

September 8, 1850

I have Tom tied up the wagon. His father hasn't even looked at him since he got his money back.

I can understand that. If a boy of mine turned out that way, I'd think twice about owning up to him too.

I should have listened harder to Jacob. Now I can see the mean streak in that boy. Rachel shies away from him and so does that pup. If it weren't for that, I'd consider turning him loose and telling him to go to California. He's only seventeen.

There's a bad streak in him though. Nothing but a prison will cure him.

One last stop. Tomorrow we'll cross the Sandy River Toll Bridge and make our way down to Oregon City.

I talked with Drake again. He told me what I'd already guessed. This isn't the first time Tom's been in trouble. He's their youngest boy and they came to Oregon hoping he'd straighten out. It looks like that won't happen. I didn't offer to turn him loose and he didn't come out and ask.

Stealing that kind of money is a hanging offense. I pray the Lord will have mercy on him.

Sincerely,
John Andrew Harding

Letter 19

September 10, 1850
Oregon City, Oregon Territory

Dear Friend,

We're in Oregon City now. I went looking for the sheriff, but it took a while. They don't have a proper jail yet and the sheriff had gone fishing.

Our camp is on the Williamette River. Watkins is still with us and so is the Thomas family. It didn't take us long to find Tyler either.

We have to look over the land, find some that isn't claimed, and stake it. It's got to be good land with good water and enough of it that Jim can settle next door. It might take me a while.

At least we're here. The children need new shoes since they've walked the soles off their old ones. I'd like to find a good hotel with a real bathtub. Al Thomas has the same thought so we'll trade off our children.

Thomas, Watkins and I went down to the land deed office together. If we can manage to be neighbors, it will help out.

September 13, 1850

Now I'm feeling civilized again. My trail beard is gone and most of the dirt too. Emily was happy to see the beard gone and we had a fine night in a real bed. There are a couple of bath houses here and some decent barbers. Emily is determined to get the children clean too.

We've found a stretch of land on the Williamette that might work. It's more than two days away and further south, but there's enough of it. Thomas and I will ride down there as soon as the Drake trial is done. They'll need me at the courthouse for that. I'd better take Jacob with me, but the women don't have to go.

September 15, 1850

News just came from the states that President Taylor is dead and Milliard Fillmore has been president since July. I don't care for that. Fillmore is a lawyer from New York. There's nothing I can do about it, but I wish he was a military man.

They hung Tom Drake too. I didn't go to the hanging. Now I can put that behind me. If they had let Tom go, it wouldn't have been over.

September 19, 1850

The land checked out. There's good water and good lumber for building. I also found two meadows we won't have to clear so we can start planting there. Al Thomas found a place too. There's already the beginnings of a road through there and he'll be across and down a bit. I just wish Jim were here so I could get his opinion. I can file on almost three thousand acres using my money and Jim's. We'll need to get a surveyor to set our property lines and make it legal.

September 23, 1850

Jim is here! You could have knocked me over when he drove his wagon into our camp. Elizabeth was looking fair, but I didn't need to ask to know that the baby didn't live. They brought a couple of other surprises with them though.

The Ross children are trail orphans. The boy, Sam, is seven and the little girl is Tessa. She's two years old. Folks took care of them after they lost their parents and gave them to the doctor at Fort Boise. It didn't take long for him to ask Jim and Elizabeth to take them. They lost everything along with their parents.

It's a good thing. The boy knows his parents are dead and he's happy to be with Jim. The girl probably won't remember them. Elizabeth has children finally and they'll do. Jim will have to take them in front of the judge to give them his name, but he'll get that done.

Now we can get our claims done and start building on our own land.

Your friend,
John Harding

Letter 20

October 10, 1850
The Homestead

The surveyor finally got round to us. With so many people coming in, he's one busy fellow. There are a dozen others at work around the territory, but Blake came recommended and everyone else was just as busy.

We haven't been waiting. We left the women in camp at Oregon City and came on down. That was a good thing too because others had their eyes on this land and we had to explain we'd filed and were just waiting for the surveyor. In the meantime we are felling logs and notching them. We might have enough for a cabin soon.

We're not the only one needing the surveyor. Thomas has his land picked out and there's Jim's and mine. Watkins is also here, but he's getting just four hundred acres. His health is none too good and he's got plans to build a store and rooming house. Once we get a school and a church, we'll have the beginnings of a town.

October 15, 1850

We got our deeds today and can finally move everyone on to our own land. Some of our oxen are gone. Emily got a good price for them and picked us up a milk cow that was still fresh.

My smart girl found herself some chickens and I settled up with the owner today so she could start her own flock. Lura didn't like chickens back in Tennessee, but I think the trail has changed her mind about their usefulness.

We'll have to come up with some sort of school too. Between our two families and the Thomas family we've got eight children that need schooling now and four more later. It's a good thing we brought our own schoolmarm because we're going to need her. As soon as we get a place built where she can teach, Elizabeth will start. She might get a few other students too. Back in the states they wouldn't let a married woman teach, but no one is going to mind that here. Teachers are rare and children have to be taught.

We're going to be real busy in the upcoming months and I'm not sure when I'll get another chance to write to you. It's time I gave you a proper goodbye so you'll know not to look for more letters. It's been a pleasure doing it, but this is goodbye.

Your friend,
John Harding

AUTHOR'S NOTE

Now that you have completed the journey through the eyes of John Harding, you should know you can also read it from Lura's point of view (**Lura's Oregon Trail Adventure**), Jacob's point-of-view (***Jacob's Oregon Trail Adventure***) or Emily's point-of-view in the upcoming **Mrs. Harding's Oregon Trail Adventure**.

Why four books? Originally the idea was to send personalized letters through the mail to children getting *Letters Through Time*. That was successful, but I lacked the money to make it a business in the 1990s. I had requests for the parents' books after releasing the two children's and I admit I had great fun going deeper into the lives of the Hardings. For John I absolutely had to know what kind of guns he had and what phase the moon was in any time he remarked on the moon. If you go to the NASA website, you can find that information for any date. Emily's book will include a few of her recipes and some she collected on the trail. I'll also have to make a clothing inventory because she will want to know. John could laugh off his son coming back caked with mud, but Emily is aware those clothes need to be at least brushed before they get back into the wagon.

I am going to let her introduce herself now.

AN INTRODUCTION TO EMILY HARDING

March 1, 1850
Greenfield, Tennessee

Dear Friend,

You don't know me, but my name is Mrs. John Harding. You can call me Emily. I was asked to write to you by this lady up in Martin. I think she might know your family. She asked because I told her we are packing to move to Oregon. I admit it would be nice to write about our journey and so I agreed to it. I hope you don't mind. There's no need to reply since I am sure the mail will never catch up with us.

This week my husband, John, sold our pitiful little farm. It wasn't producing much and the bank was going to take it soon if we didn't sell out. He got a good price for our hundred acres and we are going to use it to move to Oregon.

It's a pretty big job since everything we are taking must fit into our farm wagon. That's only five feet wide and ten feet long. John is insisting we take the harpsichord since he loves to hear me play it. I'd like my table and chairs. They belonged to my mother and she gave them to me as a wedding gift. I didn't get anything else so practical!

You see, I came from a genteel family in Kentucky. My father was a banker and well respected. My mother was known for her charity. The Graysons of Louisville were not quite rich, but

I went to a fine finishing school and my sister married well. I didn't, but I married the man I wanted.

John Harding is tall, nearly six foot, and nicely built. He's a hard-working man too and has no reason on this earth to be ashamed of anything. The instant I looked up at him, I knew he was the one for me. That's no light thing because I am cursedly tall. Mother despaired of my ever getting married because no one in our class wanted such a tall wife. That's why she, at least, approved of John. Father did too after a time. He could recognize worth. When John asked for me, he was none too happy about it though.

Well, that was nearly sixteen years ago. I have three lovely children and have not regretted giving up silks for calico. I won't regret giving up this farm either. It's too small for us and worn out. Oregon land is supposed to be rich and plentiful. It will be a good change.

Of course, the girls are still in shock. Jacob is taking it in stride. He didn't like parting with his bay mare, but when he learned his father was also selling Banner, his Morgan stallion, he put a good face on it. Lura is starting to see it as adventure, but little Rachel is still crying over the friends she will never see again. John has suggested we leave her behind to come out next year with her Aunt Elizabeth, but Elizabeth has no intention of staying behind. I've tried to tell John that, but the menfolk are determined not to take a woman in a delicate condition on the trail. As if that mattered! Babies get born no matter where the mothers are. And I think Elizabeth will carry this baby better if she knows where her man is instead of fretting over whether he is alive or dead.

I have to admit I want Elizabeth to go. I don't need help with the children, but I would like her company. It is so much better when you have kin to rely on for those little things the menfolk shouldn't have any part of. Cooking and cleaning go faster, too. We just have to convince our husbands that taking her on the trail will be better than leaving her behind. Once that's settled, there will be no question on Rachel.

I must sort linens now and decide what to take. I think I can probably sell the fancy ones I've never used. I got such a lot of those when I married. I will keep one fine dress. It's hopelessly out of style, but my blue silk was what John first saw me in and he is really partial to it. I can still wear it, but I do have to cinch the corset tighter these days.

Have you got a dress you can't bear to part with?

I must pack.

Sincerely yours,
Mrs. John Harding

ABOUT THE AUTHOR

Ellen Anthony is the author of the *Letters Through Time* series, the Syran novels, and the Jasper Stone mysteries. In 2020 she packed her car and took off. Traveling 5400 miles through 10 states, she only stopped when the lockdown hit. Her characters tracked her down and she continues to write from an undisclosed location in Oregon. Reviews are most appreciated.

The *Letters Through Time* series
Lura's Oregon Trail Adventure
Jacob's Oregon Trail Adventure
Mr. Harding's Oregon Trail Adventure
Mrs. Harding's Oregon Trail Adventure *(pending 2025)*